Chokora!
A Kenyan Scavenger

PGN Mbugwa

Nsemia

Nsemia Inc. Publishers

First Edition: November 2014
Published by Nsemia Inc. Publishers (www.nsemia.com);
Oakville, Ontario, Canada

Edited By: Charles Phebih-Agyekum
Cover Concept & Illustration: Robert Maina
Cover Design: Danielle Pitt
Layout Design: Kemunto Matunda

Note for Librarians:
A cataloguing record for this book is available from
Library and Archives Canada.

ISBN: 978-1-926906-42-3

DEDICATION

To all that endure the harsh police cell conditions

About the Author

PGN Mbugwa was born in Thika Town, 40 km from Nairobi. He attended Starehe Boy's Centre and Saint Mary's School in Nairobi. On completing high school, he joined the Kenya Air Force (KAF) and graduated as a 2nd Lieutenant in 1990. He later retired from the Armed forces and moved to South Africa. It is during his stay down south that he discovered a passion for the written word and has ever since been pursuing writing as a vocation. *Chokora! A Kenyan Scavenger* is his first novel, which won the 2nd runners up prize in the 2009 National Book Development Council of Kenya Literary award. Peter is married with a daughter and two sons.

Epilogue

John Patrick Njeri and Martin Joseph Atieno sat in the dock of Court Number 1 at the Makadara Law Courts looking dazed and scared. The yet-to-heal bruises on their faces, coupled with their youthful features, made a pitiful appearance of the duo.

Basoli and Sumo also occupied the same bench, but their facial expressions were a stark contrast, for theirs was a contemptuous countenance oblivious of the predicament they found themselves in. Simply said: the latter two were in familiar surroundings.

Gathimba wa Kamau sat with head bowed in submission. He occasionally shook his head with regret. Missing from the cast was Naomi Njoki, who was still in custody at the Jogoo Road Police Station awaiting interrogation.

Reality had finally dawned on John and Martin. Their mothers had failed to turn up at the police station the previous day and, as promised by the Officer Commanding the Station (OSC), they were now at the mercy of the court.

It was 7.00 am. Court sessions here usually started at around 9.00 am. It had been an agonizing morning for the youthful suspects. At the police station, they had been woken up at 5.00 am in preparation for court attendance. Man Kariz was on hand to wish them well, with his usual tools of trade: a bucket full of tea and loaves of bread. A quick roll call and the five were bundled into a waiting police vehicle.

The holding cells at the Makadara Law Courts were crowded with inmates arriving from various police stations in the jurisdiction. It was a desirable break to sit in the dock away from all the hassle and bustle of the holding cells with hardly any space for oneself; at least here in the dock, one had the comfort of sitting on a wooden bench.

A sizeable crowd had already gathered in the courtroom, composed mainly of friends and relatives of the accused persons. John and Martin kept peeping across the room, but could not make out any familiar face from those assembled. For the duo, it all seemed to be gloom and doom.

The presiding magistrate took her seat at exactly 9.00 am. Her demeanour was of the no-nonsense type, projecting a contemptuous glare at the 'criminals' standing in the dock. Basoli and Sumo, appearing cowed by her presence, stood with faces bowed in fear. After the usual court procedures, the case of robbery with violence against Basoli and Sumo was mentioned. The duo denied the charges. The magistrate without a glance remanded the two for two weeks, pending the mention of their case after one week.

Gathimba wa Kamau was next to be called out. He was also remanded but had the option of being released on a cash bail of Ksh. 50,000 while awaiting the mention of his case.

"Your honour, as to the charges facing John Patrick Njeri and Martin Joseph Atieno, the complainant in this case has decided not to press charges against the two. Subsequently the state has decided to drop the charges," said the court prosecutor.

CHAPTER ONE

A bold sound of steel doors being forcefully closed and locked is another noisy crushing blow sealing my fate. I am in prison. My face feels bruised and swollen, as my tongue licks blood off my balloon-like swollen lips. A sour taste of saliva and blood mix smothers my entire mouth. This is all as a result of the brutal beating I endured in the hands of security guards working at Grazers Academy in Buru Buru estate. I am in a selfish reverie, absorbed in painful body agonies, and fearing the dim reality of the future ahead that I am totally unaware of my accomplice, 'Marto'.

The mere thought of Marto further weakens my knees. I am his mentor. I personally recruited him from the slime and mire of cleaning animal waste in trucks transporting goats from northern Kenya. He was only nine years old then. Today at fifteen, he is experiencing life in a jail cell, courtesy of my tutelage.

I always preach to him saying, "I am Invincible, we will never ever be caught!" convincing him I have the answer to all his dreams. "Sooner than later", I would confidently assure him, "we'll say goodbye to the horrendous settlements of Huruma."

Unfortunately my exploits and schemes have put us both in a police cell, charged with breaking and entering a private school.

My guilt-spiced pains are no consolation to my predicament. I am only seventeen and in jail, although it is my first time. Martin is crouched beside me; he has also suffered a similar beating ordeal, courtesy of the merciless guards at Grazers Academy. Though younger than me, Martin has a big body physique for his age. I am tall, with a slender structure.

*****

After booking us, the police officer a Constable Rotich (name gleamed from his name tag) violently bundles us into the cells. He hurls insults at us as he shoves us inside.

"*Na mkae gaangarri! Msiolewe huko ndani!*" Rotich speaks in a voice laced with malice, warning us to put up a brave show or not be 'married' by sexual perverts in the cells.

At the moment we are in the corridor leading to the holding cells. The walls are littered with all kinds of graffiti"

Osama was here!

I repair broken hearts!

Judges love to wear dresses and wigs!

These writings on the walls are a worthwhile distraction from my distress.

Voices can be heard coming from the holding cells. The corridor, a mere metre wide, is dimly lit, with a bulb high up on the roof, about 20 feet above.

Negative thoughts cloud my mind about the reception awaiting us in the holding cells.

"I must wear a mean, mature mask, on my face to survive in this dungeon," I say to myself. Looking at my associate, he is still engrossed and squatting in a posture of self pity: head between legs, hands routinely massaging head.

Before I can offer Marto some consolation, a black, bald head suddenly shoots out from the holding cell, mouth wide open, and forehead glittering.

"New ones!! *Manew* ones!!" he yells emerging to investigate our arrival. His body structure drowns any attempts of bravery on my part. The guy is over 6 ft tall with a killer mask for a face.

"*Ni chokora!!*" screams a new voice also in the welcoming party. The mention of the derogatory name *chokora!* awakes my survival instincts.

"Yes! I am. I am a *chokora!*" It is my trade, camouflaged, I roam the city neighbourhoods scavenging: shabbily dressed, dirty appearance and carrying a sack on my shoulder.

How I hope other inmates will treat us with contempt as is the norm in the outside world. Gruesome tales of the torturous life in jails keep flushing through my mind.

"*Ni! Machokora! Aaah! Machokora!*" Adds the first inmate, his voice a brutal bark.

*****

"*Wee! Amkaa!*" He growls at Martin to stand up and unleashes a lethal kick aiming at his ribs. Martin is still crouched in his miserable posture. I immediately jump to Martin's defence.

"*Mmsare! mwaache!*" I plead for my friend to be left alone. My defensive audacity is received with awe and disgust by the duo.

"Sumo! Sumo!" butts in the second inmate.

"*Hawa ma-chokosh wanakujua wewe ni nani hapa ndani?*" He wonders if we really understand Sumo's stature in this enclosure, and is so perturbed by my guts.

"*Ninyi ni mafalaa wa mtaa gani!?*" Sumo demands to know our neighbourhood as his massive, sweaty fingers violently go for my throat, throttling me in the process!

My mention of Huruma as my *mtaa*, seems to catalyze his anger.

"*Basoli!! Basoli! Umesikia?? Ati! Huruma ndiyo mtaa! Huruma! Hatuna huruma sisi!*". He howls hatred, over Huruma my neighbourhood, as his spit drizzles all over my face and swearing to show us no mercy.

"*Hii* Police station *ni ya ma-boys wa Jeri, Ofaro, Salem, Mbote au Baha, Huruma utaitisha transfer kutoka kwa OCS hatuwataki hapa!*" Sumo loudly lists the neighbourhoods which hold the 'rights' to be caged in this police station and thereafter declares us *persona non grata* in a vicious voice. Abruptly walks back to the cell.

"*Mmesikia Sonko vile amebonga?*" says Basoli, the other inmate whose joy is to stir up the drama. He warns us his boss is unhappy with a Huruma presence in 'their' cells.

"*Ama mna kitu kidogo niwatetee?*" He solicits money, with a corrupt cry 'something small to grease my palms' while cracking his knuckles threateningly. He is certainly a side-kick of Sumo. His looks and sounds tell it all.

Basoli is of average height, neither too tall nor too short. He is fat and has facial features which resemble a childhood bully who I always wish never to encounter again.

He extorts, as Sumo terrorizes their domain, Jogoo police station, in the east of the City.

"*Fasta! kama mna kitu!*" His patience appears shaky, telling me to speed on a bribe. I have a two hundred bob note, secretly stashed within me, but am not willing to part with the whole amount. Surely I do not foresee getting a rebate from either Basoli or Sumo.

"*Nina soo moja*" I offer to part with a hundred shillings. My offer of a hundred bob renews the shine on Basoli's face. He smiles from ear to ear, while pulling me aside from Marto.

"*Soo moja!*" he repeats my offer as if doubting that I have the said amount of money on me.

"*Soo moja sote wawili na hatutaki noma,*" I repeat my offer of a hundred shillings while gesturing inclusively, towards Marto. I am bargaining for a peaceful coexistence with the duet.

Basoli tagging close by and nagging me to hand over the cash is emitting a nauseating, stale stench from his mouth. His stale body odour complements the smell from the cell toilets making me shiver and shudder at the prospect of living with this stink and sting.

"*Chota! fasta! fasta! Ama mlale kwa choo leo!*" Basoli's anger is mounting and orders me to close the deal or we sleep in the toilets.

His threat that we spend our first night in the jail toilet is revolting and obnoxious. I immediately fish out the money. He grabs the cash with greed and glee. He glides off into the cells without even a second glance at us or checking the cash. His acceptance drill sends a scary thrill through my stomach and I feel hard pressed to use the toilet but the foul smell deters me from rushing there.

"Marto!" I reach out to my friend and help him up, onto his feet. We have to join the others in the holding cells. The stink of the toilets from our position here is unbearable. I am praying for a fresh break once inside the cells.

As we stagger inside, I see four other inmates. I cannot fail to notice a smartly dressed gentleman standing in deep meditation gazing at the wall on the right corner of the cell. On the immediate left corner a guy lies huddled on the bare surface. He is sleeping like a baby.

On the opposite left corner, Sumo and Basoli are seated on the floor, busy conversing in hushed tones. Our entry startles them both. Their part of the cell is covered by a piece of worn out blanket and a large cardboard, the only existing evidence of beddings to be found in this police cell. The rest of the cell is cold concrete.

"*Mtalala ile kona!*" Basoli points out where we are to spend the night. The cell is a 12 ft by 12 ft cubicle with a high roof and a small metal grill for a window. A heavy steel door remains open and a lone bulb on the rooftop is on, although it's daytime. We take our place which is diagonally opposite the welcoming duo.

Inside the cell is humid, poorly ventilated, offering no relief to the suffocating smells within and without. Settling down, I eagerly anticipate the pair will play friendly. All I can think about is my 200 shillings.

"I hope they give me a refund," a monetary thought crosses my mind as I attempt a smile on swollen lips.

"*Saa ngapi!! Wee! Wewe! Saa ngapi?*" Sumo wants to know the time, now rising from his corner and addressing the well-clad gentleman facing the wall opposite us.

"Manager!! *Sonkoo!! Wee! Manager! Time?*" Sumo asks again, with a demanding swagger.

The 'Manager' slowly turns and I notice he is intimately holding on to a bottle of water. As he takes a swig of the liquid, I cannot refute Sumo's assertions, *he is a Manager.* Smart, serious, he plays the role.

The 'Manager' extends out his left wrist and displays a dazzling Casio watch, and in a demeaning attitude responds "It is 11 am Saturday the 13th of January".

"*Na Mwaka! Mwaka, unatakakujua?*" He asks sarcastically, if he should also tell the year and gulps down the water.

"*Huyu fala! Niini! Basoli! Basoli!!? Elezea huyu fala mimi ni nani !?*" Sumo growls in anger at the 'Manager' for his irony, asks Basoli to caution the 'Manager'. He is dangerous as the worst.

It had not occurred to me that everyone had one shoe on except the 'Manager' who has both shoes on and a wrist watch. No wonder he looks so glorious, 'shiny shoes' in a police cell, and dressed in a business suit.

Before all my senses can fully acclimatize with this new surroundings, the clinging sound of metal doors being opened interrupts thoughts and movement then, pin-drop silence, within the cell.

All spot subdued expressions on their faces; Sumo`s gaze resembles dried, smoked fish. I cannot help it, but am all smiles and giggles!

"Jeff Riga! Jeff, Jeff!!" Rotich is calling out a name, sadly, it is not Martin or Patrick.

"*Ndiyo mkubwa!*" replies the 'Manager' walking out. A fresh breeze flows in as the main cell door is opened making me yearn for freedom.

The guy we found snoozing soundly is now awake with hands gently massaging his naked toes trying to orientate himself, while marvelling at Marto and me. "New ones! New ones!! he says nodding his head continuously, eyes saggy and sleepy.

Sumo and Basoli appear lost at the departure of our 'Manager'. Sumo had being brazing for a brawl moments before Rotich interrupted him.

"*Usijali Sumo, haka kabuda kanarudi, kesi yake ni ya* rape" Basoli assures of the 'Manager's' return with a malicious grin deforming his face. Basoli reveals the 'Manager' is being held for rape.

"Basoli! *Sasa! Mambo yangu vipi?*" I break my silence, seeking the rebate from Basoli. I smile broadly hoping my enthusiasm will be contagious and soften the dubious duo.

"*Ati Nini ! Umesema nini? Mambo gani?*" Basoli shouts loudly, denying my acquaintance.

"Wewe chokora wacha wazimu za Glue sniffing! Mambo ganii! Mimi unanijua??" and both erupt into loud laughter accusing me of being a mere glue sniffing delinquent. It painfully dawns on me the two are devious scoundrels who scorn offers of friendship.

"Ma-boys! Ma-boys! Mmeshikiwa nini?" the 'lone-sleeper' speaks, curious of our arrest. His question makes me turn to Marto. I am surprised! Marto is already enjoying a nap, with his body curved on the bare surface like a snake.

I must create alliances here, so I welcome the lone-sleeper's question with gusto! "Breaking and Entering!" I say to him. In a way suggesting the offence is rather petty as I have been through worse.

"Wapi? Mlishikwa wapi?" He probes the whereabouts of our arrest.

"Buru-Buru, Grazers Academy," I answer him.

"Kulienda how? *Hebu nielezee!!"* the lone-sleeper persists; he is hungry for details of our offence. It is painted on his entire face.

The dirty duo are still seated in their 'sacred' corner enjoying, a cigarette. I notice they are eavesdropping on our conversation. I lick my bruised bulgy lips to hide a mischievous grin. "Narration of my ordeals will shame their banditry endeavours," I promise myself and the lone-sleeper here seems an attentive audience.

Fortunately today I am all tied up from going scavenging, and under these present circumstances am certain Constable Rotich will be screening all my visitors.

CHAPTER TWO

"*Huruma, ndiyo Mtaa!!*'," I begin. "*Huruma ni nghetto! Huko ni nghetto!*" the lone-sleeper reminds me the poor status of my neighbourhood, his accent betraying his ethnic background. Huruma, is a poorly planned, dusty and congested settlement north-east of our city. It is obvious why the lone-sleeper refers to it as a Ghetto.

"I curse Huruma for all these," I continue my narration. "Why was I, born there? This self censure question can only be answered by my father," I continue, adjusting my sitting posture to enhance my comfort on the chilling surface.

"I have never, ever, seen the man and my single mother never utters his name!" I pause before continuing,

"My *Cucu* talks bitterly of an Air Force Officer from the neighbouring military base who she reckons is my father. He went absent without a word before I was born. Cucu has also raised my mother solo. She is a widow. Her 'come-we-stay husband', a soldier in the nearby barracks, died in the line of duty. Cucu was only three months into her pregnancy. She never ceases to remind my mother the hardships she faced raising her.

"In school, I lacked the basics: rubber, ruler, pen and my uniform was often in tatters. Such a beginning is the basis of me being here. I began my studies at a school in the heart of Huruma, Tana Primary School." The lone-sleeper is all ears listening with a hypnotic stare.

Marto is still enjoying his nap, occasionally wriggling and muttering inaudible words. The desperate pair appears bored and lost, but, still tuned in to my story.

"In my class, there were fifty students packed in a room normally housing a maximum of thirty."

The now familiar sound of steel doors opening jolts my story session. I am all ears, hoping for a call to salvation from Rotich.

I do not wait long, in comes the 'Manager'. Jeff Riga, looks tortured and tormented, his absence must have had a negative impact to his countenance, the 'Manager' is emaciated. He immediately takes his position directly opposite us and adopts the popular posture of self pity, sitting with head between lower limbs and upper limbs routinely caressing head.

The return of the 'Manager' awakens the diabolical spirits of Sumo and his sycophant for they are now pacing around the cell plotting their next move.

"*Twende tukachome kwa choo,*" Sumo motions Basoli as they head off to the toilets to smoke weed. I am scared of their comeback from inhaling hemp in the midst of toxic toilet fumes.

"*Mimi ni Gathimba wa Kamau,*" says the lone-sleeper and contemptuously ignores the departing couple. His eagerness for my story casts a suspicious doubt on his motives.

"*Niiite Gathimba,*" he further urges me to feel free and call him by his first name. "*Wamenishika ati mimi ni mungiki,*" lamenting over his arrest. He is alleged to belong to an illegal notorious sect but swears his innocence. He works as a tout at the city bus terminus.

"*Endelea na story, imenibamba no-ma!*" Gathimba urges me to reveal more. "*Ninyi ni ma-junior, mmefika huku aje?*" astonished at how young we are.

My mouth is dry, sore and salty; the only water available is in the toilets. Jeff is clutching onto another water bottle, his precious tight grip on the bottle puts off anyone daring enough to beg for a swig. I have to brush off this thirst notion and build bridges before the blazing brats return from their inferno.

I am flattered by Gathimba's enthusiasm on my escapades and I confidently continue my tale with a nostalgic recall of my primary school days.

"Fifty in a class with only one Teacher, it is common to find three students balancing their behinds, on one chair. Majority of children in my school are from the slums adjoining Huruma. A combination of hell bent mixture of characters, I presume poverty is a potent ingredient for our social decadence. During my first day in school I lost everything: bags, books, save for me."

Sumo and Basoli storm back, stinking and stoned. They are a merry two-some as they occupy their warm spot.

"*Sonko! Anakaa kama simba imenyeshewa,*" jokes Basoli, pointing at Jeff's posture which he equates to a rain-soaked lion. The pair laughs lavishly and irritatingly. Jeff Riga shrugs off this excitement and sits engrossed in self-empathy. I remain quiet, waiting for the jolly duet to ease on their sarcasm.

"*Endelea wewe na story!*" says an impatient-sounding Gathimba, pressing me to carry on with my narration.

"*Wewe Mungiki nyamaza!*" retorts Sumo, glaring menacingly at Gathimba, who also stares back with equal menace.

Watching Gathimba and Sumo from where I sit, a sinking feeling drains all blood from my head. I feel dizzy, dreading a brewing hostility.

Suddenly! Gathimba leaps up like a wild cat fronting for a fight.

"Nani? Mungiki?" He confronts Sumo for linking him to the outlawed outfit. Sumo is least intimidated by Gathimba's bravado.

Sumo takes cue, and is on his feet.

Gathimba is down, with a thud!

Sumo has knocked him out with a powerful punch. Sumo is fast and furious. Martin and Jeff are now wide awake startled by the ensuing fracas.

Basoli is on his legs motivating Sumo to reign supreme and whitewash the opposition.

"Mgeuze duster!" Basoli cheers, rooting for Sumo to flatten his victim mercilessly. Gathimba is pinned to his corner with Sumo landing lethal blows at will.

Wow! Like the proverbial 'cat with nine lives' Gathimba slips out of the cell in lightning speed.

"Atalala choo leo!!" quips Sumo panting heavily, avows Gathimba will spend the night in the toilets. He and his hanger-on remain standing.

Their brutal bashing of Gathimba has boosted their egos. They trot back and forth, towering over the three of us, humbled by their debacle. Sumo is sniffing for any hints of discontent.

"Kuna mwingine?" he issues a challenge.

"Niko Hapa! Nimerudi!" It is Gathimba announcing his resurgence.

Martin, Jeff and I instinctively spring up onto our feet. Gathimba is a pathetic portrait to behold! All cringe and crowd in Jeff's corner in a bid to escape from him. The purported member of a proscribed cult is smeared in human waste, from the waist up. Chest bare, he carries a handful of the waste, daring the offending two to a face off. There is nowhere to hide.

"Mshike! Basoli mbambe! Shika huyu wazimu!" Sumo barks, ordering Basoli to restrain him and attempting to use us to shield himself against Gathimba's wrath. Basoli is not willing to wrestle

with Gathimba and ignores Sumo's orders. The familiar sound of steel doors opening provides us with the desired break. Gathimba is unmoved by the unlocking doors, still prompting the pair to step out of their cover.

"Leo ni leo, mtakula mavi!!" he vows loudly that somebody must sample his 'sumptuous' scoop.

This filthy remark clearly reverberates through out the police station as the main door leading out of the cells is open. Before we can savour his threats, a gorgeous lady appears on the door way. All attention quickly shifts. Her alluring presence has also bamboozled Gathimba off his tracks. Head turned, he delights at the one bare footed beauty.

The 'Beauty' freezes in fear at the caricature before her eyes. Thereafter, she turns back vomiting, choking and crying out aloud.

"Iko nini! What is happening?"

"Ati mtakula nini!" Rotich voices his concern over Gathimba's blurts, pushing forward the lady as he appears and stands by the doorway. He is also tongue tied and terrified by the atrocious scene. He reacts fast, and closes the cell door, leaving us at the mercy of Gathimba, unlocking the opposite cell and pushing in, the 'beautiful one'.

"Mrembo! Karibu maskani!" Rotich welcomes her to the new surroundings and padlocking her cell door from the outside.

A grill opening on cell doors enables me to view her new quarters.

"Are you crazy? You smell like a skunk!" Rotich shouts through the grill opening. *"Nini mbaya hapa?"* he questions the fiasco. *"Na rudi kwa* roll-call, *nikupate umeoga! Fisi wewe!!"* he warns Gathimba to clean up. Rotich walks away but leaves the cell door open.

"Wacha, muhadhara bestee!!" Sumo softens his stance towards Gathimba.

"Tuliza ball, uwanja mdogo," Basoli tries to cool tempers.

"Bestee!! Sasa! Sisi nii Mabeste?" Gathimba is cynical of their truce offer.

"Nataka mwachane na mimi!!" He demands to be left alone.

"Mambo poa, enda uoge; dumisha usafi," Sumo reassures him all is well and emphasizes the advantages of keeping clean.

I yawn and take a long breath of relaxation as Gathimba departs for a makeover. I am proud of him; he has contained the rogues within by reciprocating their uncouth deeds.

"We! wewe fala wa Huruma, wewe ndio umeleta hii noma!" Basoli snarls, shifting the blame on me. We meekly take our spot in the cell gripped by fear but presenting brave faces.

"Wacha hawa mafala wa Huruma!" Sumo opts to ignore Basoli's incitement remarks about us.

"Kiboko yao iko motoni!" he warns of a painful payback, which he is concocting for Martin and I.

CHAPTER THREE

BANG!! BOOM!! And we are all petrified out of our wits. The paralyzing sounds are coming from the main door leading out of the cells. Constable Rotich is opening the steel doors. From the sound and style with which he goes about the task, the policeman is not a happy person.

"Fall in!! *Kila mtu nje!*" Rotich orders all to assemble outside the cells. I am out first and observe that he is holding the Big Book where he wrote down our names. We all fall into a single line except the *beauty*, still locked in her cell. I eagerly wait for the 'beautiful one' to emerge. Oooh! My eyes twitch, desperate to feast on her gorgeous sculpture.

"*Sikiza jina lako!*" Rotich starts calling out names from the register. "Walter Thomas Aduda alias Sumo'?"

"*Niko afande!*" answers Sumo in aloud voice.

"*Niko na swali afande! Tunaenda kortini lini?*" Sumo complains they have been held up in these cells for too long and wish to be taken to court

"Paul Stanely Midau alias Basoli," Rotich ignores Sumo's sentiments and continues his check on the register.

"*Niko afande!*"

"John Patrick Njeri!"

"*Niko afande!*" I answer shyly, embarrassed at my surname. Rotich, when booking us, had insisted we all must have three names.

"Martin Joseph Atieno!".

"Present sir," Martin replies, reluctantly accepting his last name.

17

"Jeff Riga Simba and John Gathimba Kamau," he calls out.

I turn around and to my surprise Gathimba is standing at the rear, all spruced up, he answers with a sparkling smile.

"Naomi Njoki!" Rotich concludes.

We all stare at the locked cell, our eyes tearing down the steel door hoping to get a candid view of the 'new one'.

"Rudi ndani ya cell! Kila mtu!" Rotich commands all to return to our holding cell. My stomach is rumbling, a signal of hunger. We all take our positions silently as Rotich walks away dashing any hopes of liberty.

"NO! No! No! This can not be real!" Jeff cries out, punching the wall angrily. He walks back and forth, within the cell muttering to himself. "Impossible, this is maliciously outrageous! I must get out of here!" he sighs and groans.

"Relax *buda! Wacha pupa!*" Gathimba reaches out to Jeff, reassuring him and tactically attempting to build a bond.

"They have vowed to finish me!" he says, maintaining his grip on the water bottle with a look of despair painted on his whole face.

"Attempted rape! *Mimi!*" He moans, refuting the alleged rape charges against him.

"Kulienda vipi?" Gathimba is now fascinated by Jeff's mention of the word rape, which sounds juicy.

I glimpse at the terrible two, and notice that Sumo has lit another cigarette. Basoli is craving for a puff, with his fingers drumming desperately across his lips and whistling tired tunes.

"Wewe ni mdosi sana!" Gathimba chats Jeff with awe, a prying stare illuminating his face. Jeff's esteem and self worth is substantially heightened by Gathimba's applause of his stature in this enclosure.

"*Leta* story *Sonko!*" Gathimba nudges Manager to tell his tale leading him here. Gathimba fidgets on the solid surface searching for a comfortable listening posture. A side glance of disdain to his right, and Jeff is raring to go. He takes a long gulp from his water bottle, which nearly empties all the contents. He saves a few drops, which he passes on to Gathimba.

"I am the Branch Manager of Stop2Shop supermarket along Jogoo road," he begins. "It is all a conspiracy, a plot hatched by my jealous work mates. *Ni wivu! Wivu mtupu! Wana wivu!*" he vehemently asserts his innocence. His mouth dries up as his tongue constantly lubricates his lips, whilst eyes blinking regularly casting a doubt on his honesty.

"I have a lovely wife and two kids. I have no desire for a stupid, ugly cashier!" Jeff says in a derogatory tone and a hideous mask for a face. "Today morning Carol, a cashier, ushers into my office cops and accuses me of attempted rape. She says it happened yesterday evening after work," he speaks rising up.

"Check me out! Look at Me!" Jeff is fully stretched out, standing tall. He invites us to be the jury and judge him by his elegance.

Jeff Riga is your typical middle level income, middle-aged executive, probably living in a three bed room bungalow in a neighbourhood like Buru-Buru. I come across his type during my rounds in estates in Eastlands. He brings thoughts of my father. That is me. I see an apparition of my father in any well-groomed man. My father is a Soldier, so it is said. Jeff's flamboyant demeanour makes me wish I had a father as smart as him. Handsome, well fed, with a clean shaven bright face. He pleads 'NOT GUILTY`.

"*Sisi woote tuko innocent, lazima cell ziwe na wapangaji!*" cuts in Sumo, declaring we are innocent victims and are here as tenants of the state. He rudely waves away Jeff's emotional virtues.

Sumo then offers Gathimba a cigarette trying to distract him from Jeff. This gesture rejuvenates Gathimba, as he accepts the gift with kisses and absolute relish. Till now, he has successfully been withholding his nicotine cravings.

"Wewe kaa chini, Sonko, chokora endelea na story." Sumo reasserts his superiority and opts for my chronicles. Gathimba is no longer a threat to Sumo's supremacy, the tobacco token has tilted alliances.

"Kweli! Junior eleza kisanga yenu," Gathimba is in agreement with Sumo, cigarette on his lips; he gets up and signals for a lighter. This changing scenario is a threat to our survival in this cage. Martin sits besides me withdrawn from the goings on as Jeff storms out of the cell, apparently to protest Sumo's disruption and dismissal of his account.

"Chokora nii paraa! Nii jaaro! Vaa-ko tupu hii!" I explain our ragged persona is all a disguise to wade through the harsh habitats of city society. I scavenge, steal, pick and beg, whatever, whenever and wherever. The trio are all ears.

"Hi! Halloo! My Angel, who dares to put you here?" Jeff's voice resonates audibly; he must be talking to the Beauty in the next cell.

"Mnamsikia?" Sumo is cautious of Jeff's intents, appearing agitated and resentful of the latter's efforts to woo Naomi.

"Huyu Sonko awache yake!!" Basoli also feels offended by Jeff's overtures towards the Beauty.

"Nimashetani wote! Wacheni wataangamia!!" Gathimba reveals the real identities of the Manager and the Beauty; alleging both to be disciples of the devil and warning us to avoid them or plunge into hell's anguish.

I continue.

"Loosing my belongings during my first day in school is devastating to my spirits. I am tempted to quit school.

"The atmosphere at Tana Primary is hostile to say the least. Bullies are a reign of brutality. An older boy violently pulled at my member as I took a lick. The diabolical act caused me excruciating pain. It made me ever afraid when using the toilets.

"My evening is bound to be bleak, How will I explain the disappearance of everything to my mother?

"On my way home, an over zealous schoolmate, older than I, ridicules my down cast walk." 'A wet Chicken! You are a Wet Rooster!' He teases. I brush off his insinuations, cursing my existence; nature is unquestionably merciless for placing me in this environment.

"'*Vipi ! Mimi ni 'On Top*','' he introduces himself, a student in class six."

"*On Top! Unamjua On Top!*" Sumo is astounded by my mention of the name. He gets up and extends a clenched fist greeting to me. I am elated at his response. He seems to revere the name.

"*O-T, ni* brother," I say as a matter of fact.

"*O-T, wa Harlem! Key-cutter ? Mlisoma na yeye*?" Basoli doubtful I am talking about the same person.

"Yes! *On-Top wa Harlem! Maskan yake ni Key-base*" I proudly correct their scepticism.

"*Ndiye ametufundisha hii* works," I upset them even more, revealing 'On-Top' as the guru behind our *chokora* facade.

*****

"On-Top, an old hand in the school, must be aware of my groom," I return to relate my past.

"'*Wamekusanya?*' On Top enquired, seeking to cheer me up. '*Hapa nii Huruma, lazima ukae ngumu,*' he reminds me our school is in a rough neighbourhood and to dwell in harmony with the rest, I ought to play hard ball. There is no room for the faint hearted. I learn it is a tradition for new students to lose their things during the first day at Tana Primary School. I was not tipped off; all those with elder siblings and friends in the school are never ripped off. On-Top is sympathetic and offers to assist. He manages to recover my school bag the next day."

"Noo-ma! On-Top! Nii noo-ma!" exclaims Martin, venerating 'O-T' further. His rekindled outlook and audible articulation of the goings on is a shocker to all. We all momentarily amazed at Martin.

BANG! CLINK CLANK! Goes the debilitating sound; all go mute.

"Hiyo ni msosi! lunch wazee!" Sumo announces food is coming. He gladly walks out to take a first glimpse of the arrival of our lunch.

CHAPTER FOUR

Constable Rotich escorts in the caterer supplying the lunch as Sumo mimic's a host.

"*Wote kwa cell moja!*" Rotich says, unlocking Naomi's cell. The luncheon is to be held in our cell and Naomi will surely be the splendour of the occasion.

"*Man Kariz! Uniite ukimaliza!*" Rotich tells the caterer to summon him after completing the feeding assignment and departs.

"*Gota! Gota! Man Kariz! Gota!*" Sumo extends the clenched fist salutation to the caterer, whose countenance resembles a jail-bird: deceitful outlook with a scarred face.

"*Endelea na works! Sumo! Gawa msosi!*" The caterer, Man Kariz, delegates his duty to Sumo who assumes his new role with sheer pleasure.

The meal, *ugali* sprinkled with chunks of cabbages, is served in washed out plastic bowls.

"*Na mna kitu huku ndani!*" Man Kariz is stirred by the captivating female lounging among six men. Meanwhile, Naomi is watching the food with a loathsome gaze, fleetingly stealing a glimpse at Gathimba. His sordid sight still lingering in her mind.

Jeff is keeping close tabs on Naomi, sitting besides her; a perverted sly grin graces his visage. The couple view the shared meal as an insult to their palates and snub their portions. Gathimba and Basoli hail this rebuff and flaunt bowls full of leftover food bounty. Marto and I immerse ourselves in savouring the cell cuisine.

"Kuja tuonane, tumalizane!" Man Kariz beckons Sumo in a rather clandestine style and both walk out, their rendezvous in the reeking toilets.

"Hizo nii mangale na maboza!!" Basoli mumbles between mouthfuls; more supply of cigarettes and cannabis, divulging the stealth exit of Sumo and the caterer. Gathimba spews out a mixture of chewed cabbages and porridge, upon Basoli's disclosure. He definitely yearns for the noxious substances. Gathimba's behaviour is appalling to all except Basoli who reciprocates with repulsion by sending similar splatter flying through the air.

Jeff seeks to soothe Naomi. She has already adopted the fashionable posture of distress: sitting with legs warming her bosom.

It is well worth to acquaint ourselves with Naomi, the grandeur of this gathering. She is stout and light-skinned, with an imposing disposition, with an attractive but crafty mask for a face. Jeff's attention has not relieved her reservations about this quagmire; she randomly sneaks a sly peep at all within this cell, trembling and wincing.

"Huyu manzi ni msupaa," Martin whispers, also dazed by the dazzling human mound.

"Umeshikiwa nini Madam?" Gathimba prods Naomi, seeking the reason for her arrest. Naomi can no longer stomach Gathimba's repugnant nature, who speaks while food gushes out of his mouth. She stomps out going back into her cell. Jeff follows close behind striving to be apologetic for the despicable company.

"Watu wameshiba?" the caterer is back wondering if we have had an ample fill of his delicacies. He collects the used bowls except Sumo's which is untouched. *"Sonko na mrembo wamekitoa wapi?"* Man Kariz is nosy, curious at the absence of Naomi and Jeff.

"*Shetanii ashindwe!*" Sumo wails in a high-pitched voice, aggravated by the missing couple, blaming Satan for Jeff's courtship schemes.

"*Usisahau milk na bread! Man Kariz, poa?*" Sumo is placing orders for foodstuffs and I suspect he is paying with my money.

"*Na kumbuka kila kitu, ngale, ngwaii, naree, milk na bread.*" Man Kariz recaps the list of items to be replenished and collects his crockery ready to signal Rotich, so as to be let out.

In the opposite cubicle, Jeff has not tired from his pursuits to appease Naomi. He has managed to get her talking, though I am not able to eavesdrop on their tête-à-tête.

"*Tuonane jioni wathii!* Supper time!" the caterer wishing us well, concludes his service tour and heads to the doors; a sharp rap on the steel has Rotich opening up.

Jeff hastens back to the cell, the familiar clatter and rattle of metal against steel forcing all to cower. Sumo is calm and collected still devouring the dull meal. The doors close without a word from Rotich, who only enters to make sure Naomi's cell is padlocked.

Jeff's hang-out with the Beauty has revitalized his attitude, his face beams positively, leaving us all intrigued by the transformation. Gathimba, picking his teeth with his fingers, cannot suppress his inquisitive nerve.

"*Wee-we! Budaa!? Huyo mbuss amebambiwa* what?" I am sure Gathimba speaks for all. Why is Naomi behind these walls?

Jeff is enchanted by the questioning frowns of our attentive faces. He warms his hands, proud he holds the ace, as relating to Naomi's incarceration.

"She is in custody, for assaulting a Mrs. Adolf Nyara," he speaks, nodding his head knowingly, wife to the proprietor of Nyara Hardware Stores along

Jogoo Road. I am well acquainted with the whole Nyara family," he continues with emphasis on the latter hoping to authenticate his expose'.

We discover Naomi is single and ever willing to mingle. She loves humming the tune of the hit song *No Romance without Finance*. Lyrics to the song have inspired all aspects of her life.

Jeff reveals that Mrs. Nyara had confronted Naomi, scolding and shaming her for engaging in forbidden liaisons with Mr. Nyara. Naomi had countered the attack, biting and beating her adversary.

"Unasema, panana ya huyo manzi hatuwezani sisi?" Sumo responds, enraged by Jeff's other implications, that none here stands a morsel chance to catch the fancy of Naomi's charming eyes.

"Ananyeta natuko jela! Gathimba utamlambisha ice-cream!" Basoli hopes to incite Gathimba into playing dirty against Naomi.

"Washa ngale Sumo! *Huyu supuu lazima atoboke kitu kidogo leo!"* Gathimba prefers monetary extraction and begs for a cigarette before swinging into action.

"Wazee, please! Wacheni noma! Sarenii manzi! Nitachota! Please?" Jeff is horrified by the plot to harass Naomi and bargains to bribe the smoking trio.

I am wary there are no permanent foes or friends here, just like in Huruma my abode. Gathimba has been adopted by the two thugs who aspire to employ his mucky tactics. My zeal to create collaborations and partnerships in this cell amounts to zero. Jeff wanders out perturbed by the hostile ambience oozing from these crude characters. The atmosphere in our cell is oppressive and stuffy. Tobacco smoke engulfs us all. The three smokers have bonded pathetically and are in a jovial mood as they watch Jeff step out.

"Sumo? Kisanga yenu ni gani?" Gathimba queries the duo's deeds, leading to their captivity. Basoli is a

cloudy picture of ecstatic bliss. He inhales deeply at a cigarette with lips curled passionately around it, as he blows smoke rings into the damp air.

"Phone! *Simu!* Black-Berry *ya nguvu!*" Sumo confesses they stole a mobile phone, shaking his glittery head and smiling cunningly.

"Tuko na wiki hapa ndani. Natamani rondema, huko ndiyo home," he grumbles they have been held here for a week. Sumo prefers prison remand, he reckons the facility there offer him 'five-star' comforts.

"Mtaa nii wapi, wathii?" Gathimba prods on, interested in their origins within the city.

"Mimi natoka Jeri na Basoli nii boy wa Ofaro!" Both were born, bred in Jericho and Maringo Estates, Sumo answers him. Coincidentally, the two locations border this police station, and are low, mid-income neighbourhoods. It is thus within their birth rights to occupy these cells and demand dues, they argue. It is their home turf, so to speak.

"Mimi kwetu nii Oyolee, nimeshikwa kwa mathree!!" Gathimba reveals. He's from Kayole and was touting for passengers at the *Muthurwa matatu* terminus when cops pounced on him. Frisking him for incriminating valuables, they discovered he was not wearing his underpants. It is his worst nightmare ever. He had woken up hurriedly and forgot to wear anything underneath his pants.

It is beyond his wildest dreams that he is in the cell for such a trivial oversight. The police handcuffed him and booked him for dressing in a manner depicting himself as an outlaw.

Jeff is back. He has been consulting with Naomi in hushed tones. The terrifying triplets are still seated, glaring anxiously at Jeff awaiting their pay off so as not to splash their dirty linen in these precincts.

"*Horse Kobole! Bamba!*" Jeff hands over a five hundred shillings note. The money hypnotizes us all. Sumo is promptly up on his two legs, receiving the buy off, his soiled fingers hasty to caress the legal tender.

Basoli and Gathimba are up, patting Sumo on his back and mesmerized by the colourful piece of paper.

"*Sasa kameiva, twendeni tukavute, wazee waiivee!*" Sumo proclaims their labours have been richly rewarded and all that remains is for the three to visit the toilets and get high. They scramble out shoving Jeff aside with obvious derision.

We watch meekly, baffled by their brute behaviour as they jostle to reach the stinking toilets. This exit portends more problems, we sit dejected, scared stiff of their homecoming.

CHAPTER FIVE

"Imbeciles! Hyenas! Crazy creatures, I will teach them a lesson," Jeff is furious over the whole face and is obviously agitated.

He soon drifts into deep thought, taking his place in the opposite corner. "I will complain to the Officer in Charge if these savages continue to suppress and oppress us" Jeff vows in an incensed voice, shaking his fist like a man in a fit. I timidly nod my head in doubtful agreement, pessimistic of this approach.

"*Kweli Sonko, hawa mafala wasukume mbele!*" Marto concurs, in a coaxing tone of voice. He is aware Jeff is the only friendly force willing to fend off the opposition.

"Young man, why are you here?" Jeff asks, turning to Martin. It is a relief I am not to retell my ordeals again.

"Water pumps, *tulisanya* water pumps," Martin reveals our craze is stealing water meters and pumps. We sneak into schools, homes and even churches. We do not spare any premises.

"I overheard your friend mention Grazers Academy in Buru Buru, are you students there?"

Martin and I burst out laughing, spontaneously. Students? At Grazers? We two? His assumptions have tickled our funny spots. We laugh uncontrollably aloud, oblivious of our woes.

"*Kwetu nii Huruma, Ghetto! Grazers ni ya mababi!*" Martin substantiates, we come from the slums of Huruma and are too poor to be students at Grazers Academy.

Our connection to the school is burglary. We were caught creeping out of the swimming pool area after pinching water pumps from their storage. We occasionally slip into the school and nick items but today the guards laid an ambush. Our battered faces are a testimony to the school sentries' rage

"Strange coincidence, my boys! My daughter is a student at Grazers Academy and I know Huruma like the back of my hand. I was a commissioned officer in the Air-Force," Jeff explains, his words arousing my persistent quest to find my father. I have this weird hunch that this alleged rapist might be the one. Unfortunately, the last time I had such a premonition, I ended up in the hands of a sexual pervert who almost molested me.

*****

I vividly remember it was a day like today, Saturday. Early morning. I am on my scavenging exploits in Buru Buru. A blue gate opens and a middle-aged man appears to dispose his garbage bag. As is customary in my vocation, I rush to be the first *chokora* to rummage through his 'fresh' dumping. The man takes a compassionate look at me and invites me into his house, urging me to abandon my grimy sack outside. I foresee heavenly blessings pour down on me. This is an opportunity to take advantage of his sympathetic nature and rip him off.

Inside the richly furnished house, portraits of my host clad in military gear grace the walls. A close scrutiny indicates the guy is a pilot in the Air Force with the rank of Captain. The serene mood within the house assures me the officer is alone. The warm-hearted, cool gentleman prepares a spectacular breakfast, and even offers me the use of his bathroom to rid me of the ragged scruffy garb and my greasy appearance. I frown at his proposal to clean my act.

Visions inundate my mind as I laze on his couch. I day dream that this is my father. I have found him. I promise to abandon my waywardness and be the best son he could ever wish for.

Alarm bells of apprehension jolt my cosiness when he hands me a cocktail glass of wine. I am only fifteen.

"Drink my son! It drowns all sorrows and washes away poor self-esteem," the Captain flies his message home. I accept the glass with reservations, but a sip of the drink and the taste is unpalatable. I reject the concoction.

"I love tea," suggesting an alternative drink.

He does not take kindly my rejection to indulge in his liquid luxuries and abruptly sits next to me.

Alas! Within moments, my dream dad is all over me, hands cuddling, stroking and undressing me. His breath emits stale alcohol fumes, which blind my resisting efforts.

Luckily, I manage to wrestle him off and scamper for safety, dashing out of the house in a bewildering flight of fear and stalling the pilot's depraved plans to abuse me. Since then, I tread with prudence in my pursuits to trace my father.

*****

"Do your parents know you are here?" Jeff empathizes with our dilemma

"*Hakuna haja, massangu ni muhadhara mbaya, mbovu!*" Martin believes we are better off on our own, he cannot involve his mother, she might advocate for his imprisonment.

"What about your fathers?" he wonders.

"*Hatuna mabudda sisi. Au Pato, unajua budda ako?*" Martin informs him we do not have fathers, asking me if I think otherwise.

Coincidentally, Mr. Nyara is also the proprietor of Grazers Academy, Jeff so reveals, promising us he will pressure Nyara to drop the case against us.

Jeff is optimistic his deliverance from this tormenting dungeon will be today. His lawyer is negotiating for an amicable settlement with the complainant. It is reason for optimism for an early departure.

"*Budda unajua Huruma vizuri?*" I am restless to interrogate him, and impatient to ascertain his whereabouts seventeen years ago.

"Huruma! Haa! Twenty years ago, I could drink on credit in all the pubs of the neighbourhood," Jeff recalls, visibly proud of his past. "Boys!! I recall girls' knees would buckle at the mere presence of a soldier. Those were the days, my boys! Those were the days and Huruma was the arena. Those were the days!" an exuberant recollection spreading a sparkling glow on his full face. Jeff's blunt admission of his lust for ladies further intensifies my inkling. He is my father, my instinct tells me.

*****

"*No Woman! No Cry! More Women! More Cries!*" sing the three hooligans joining us in the cell, their chorus sounds croaky and is comically irritating. Their dramatic entry creates a carnival-like mood in the cell. The three ramble around in merriment, reaching out to us with the clenched fist salute. I timidly adjourn my cross-examination of my supposed father owing to their discourteous interjection.

"*Wewee Junior, haujatumalizia story ya O-T!*" Sumo reminds me I have not fully detailed my relationship with On-Top. I will not hesitate to disclose all of what he desires because his chumming elation might only last for a short while.

"*O-T ni broker wa burungo, Black-Berry yeye ndiyo alii-kwachu,*" Sumo owns up, he sold the mobile phone he stole to O-T, whose key-cutting business is only a front for illicit business. He doubles up as a shylock, pawn-broker, a modern-day jack of all trades.

I continue!

"At Tana Primary School I became On-Top's pet project. He acted as my elder brother, a genuine guardian angel during those hazy days. My home in Huruma is every square metre a replica of this cubicle, but with a lower roof made of iron sheets. I share the room with mother and Cucu. On the double-deck bed sleeps mum and me, while Cucu's single bed is behind the partitioned part of the room," I relate in reference to this cell.

"He has remained a mystic for, coming to think of it, I do not know On-Top's real name. He has always been O-T since he inducted me into the *Art of Scavenging*, or as local cynics call us, *chokora!*," I continue the tale. "On-Top originally lived in Huruma, though I cannot pin-point where in particular his home was. He nonetheless never seemed to tire escorting me up to where I lived".

I notice the entire cell is under my spell, all silent and tuned-in to my narration. Sumo lights a cigarette, apparently Basoli and Gathimba wobble in their positions as they ardently sniff at the drifting smoke. I am loving the attention and, elated, I proceed.

"Weekends became my working days, tiptoeing out of the house before dawn. He taught me the essence of disguise, dirty looks and all."

"*Yeaah! paaraa! Nii jaro tupu! Nilikutana na mother na hakunimezea! Para mwisho!*" Martin disrupts me, extolling the pros of a Scavengers' camouflage. Marto pompously remembers bumping into his Mother. She offensively shoved him aside unaware it was her own son.

"*Mnasema O-T alikuwa chokora?*" Basoli speaks with misgivings. On–Top was formerly a scavenger.

"*Na chapaa! Chapaa nyinyii hupata vipi?*" Gathimba wonders how foraging through garbage can turn out to be a rewarding monetary endeavour.

"*Haaa! Heee! On-Top! Ndiye kila kitu. Ana funguo za kila kitu,*" Martin is amused by Gathimba's scornfulness of our pursuits. Martin is taking away all the limelight from me. He speaks, while we all listen.

A spirit of confession seems to transcend within this cell, making Martin disclose secrets of our work ethics.

"On-Top arms us with master keys to break into properties and steal. He later pays cash for any merchandise delivered," Martin sheds the light. On-Top coordinates our activities from his make-shift stall widely referred to as Key-Base in Harlem, a settlement sandwiched between Maringo and Jericho Estates. Our attire is beyond suspicion as most people dismiss us as dirty, glue inhaling delinquents. Unknown to many, we are a treacherous bunch.

BOOM! Clink! Clank! It is the musical sound of opening doors, again!

"Roll-call, *wazee, na* change of duty," Sumo briefs us, on what portends with the unlocking doors.

CHAPTER SIX

"Fall in! *kila mtu nje!*" Constable Rotich's voice reverberates throughout the polluted atmosphere within the cells of the police station. We herd close together on our way out, each one of us trying to be out first, but we cannot all fit through the small exit. Eventually, we line up in a single file and nobody is willing to be on the rear, close to the toilets. Gathimba appears comfortable guarding the unconducive atmosphere at the rear.

The main cell door is wide open and the reception area is in full view. A light beam from the front desk illuminates the dull corridor as a cool breeze refreshes our battered, sweat-drenched, bad odour bodies. Rotich lets out Naomi from her lone cell to grace our parade.

As Rotich peruses through the register, a picturesque figure emerges from behind him. She is dressed in a well-fitting police uniform, which accentuates her body contour configuration. The cop is tall with a chocolate complexion. She is simply a master-piece of nature's creation. Her dark, shiny straightened hair is held by a cute pony tail behind her elegant neck. Naomi appears thunder-struck by the gorgeous policewoman who towers over her.

'I passionately hope she remains on duty twenty four hours a day and seven days a week,' an illusion warms my heart.

Rotich and Constable Wakesho (name gleaned from the name tag) consult silently as they go through the register.

"Naomi Njoki! Naomi Njoki?" Wakesho calls out. "*Wewe unahanya hanya na mabwana za watu, na kisha unawauma wake zao? Karibu umtoe* Carol Nyara *pua!*" Wakesho is perturbed by Naomi's alleged assault where she almost bit off the nose of her victim as they fought over the victim's husband. "Mrs. Nyara is like a sister to me. I will make sure you suffer for your debauchery, wicked home wrecker!" Wakesho swears, her anger boiling, making her skin turn pale.

She continues!

"Because you worship men, and you cannot survive without men, I present to you these six! *Ma-boys nyama hiyo!*" Wakesho says, abandoning Naomi to the wrath of the boys and nudging us to devour her if we so wish. The two police officers walk out leaving Naomi standing in a haze of confusion amidst six crooks in a dingy police cell.

"*Mabeste! Nimesikia mkibonga juu ya On-Top?*" Naomi speaks in a beseeching tone. All gaze at her, amazed to hear a soft, friendly voice inquiring about O-T.

Sumo jumps at this opportunity to home in on Naomi. He ceremoniously ushers her into our cell, constantly bowing as a show of desire for her attention. We all enter the cubicle eager to learn about Naomi's links with this mysterious On-Top.

She avoids Sumo's luring antics and drifts towards Jeff, finally settling next to him in the opposite corner.

"*On-Top ni bro wangu mdogo!*" Naomi drops a bombshell saying On-Top is her younger brother.

The revelation stuns me beyond comprehension.

Sumo lights a cigarette and generously offers the same to Basoli and Gathimba. Naomi's disclosure has jerked his nerves as well.

'On-Top is the younger brother to Naomi?' a question rings in my head as I suspiciously examine

Naomi for any proof of resemblance. This drives me more into a muddle of confused similarities.

"*Tulizaliwa Huruma. O-T jina lake ni* Simon Mwamba," Naomi enlightens us on the mystic's real name. "*Simo! Ndiyo alinishikanisha na huyu Dosi wangu,*" Naomi reveals On-Top introduced her to her current covetous 'hobby', Mr. Nyara. "O-T is also a pimp, coordinating call girls from his Key-base in Harlem," Naomi slyly whispers.

Naomi Njoki and Simon Mwamba, alias On-Top, were raised by their single mother in the slums of Huruma.

"Simon began fending for himself early in life. Mum was always absent, providing cheap labour whenever opportunity arose. We were poor with no father. Our mum cleaned homes and worked the laundry in the eastern suburbs of Nairobi," Naomi continues, recalling their early childhood.

"Our mother's toils to provide for us tormented Simon and I. He would rise before dawn and dress in tattered clothing, making him incognito before roaming the Eastland's suburbs scavenging for whatever valuables he came across. Later, our mother passed away forcing us to move from Huruma to Harlem. We moved in with our grandmother. Simon did not go to high school after graduating from Tana Primary School while I dropped out in form three. I was a student at Victoria Girls' High School in Buru Buru. Long story short ... it later dawned on me that men were willing to spend their fortunes for my attention and as the saying goes, the rest is history. Here I am," Naomi paints a promiscuous self-portrait.

"Simon is equally a shrewd schemer. Within no time he has graduated from the trash bags into a real wheeler dealer within Harlem and its environs. Now at twenty-two, my younger brother plots and trades with the likes of Mr. Nyara. Soo! If Miss Police Beauty Queen here attempts to flip me like a pinball she will lick clean these stinking toilets, d*aaa!*" *N*aomi brags, sounding rather snobbish, while striving to maintain a brave face to defy Wakesho's threats.

Sumo and Basoli rise from their positions and extend the clenched fist salutation to Naomi.

"*Gota! Gota! Kumbe wewe ni manzi waa mtaa!*" Basoli excitedly exclaims. He feels honoured she comes from his neighbourhood.

"*Kwangu nii Buruu, Harlem nishaa hama!*" Naomi denies she resides in the same location, having moved to a more affluent abode in Buru-Buru.

"*Madam! Hapa ni home, On-Top ni wetu njoo! Usijali panana za huyo sansee, ana wivu na wewe!*" Sumo wisely assures Naomi, to regard these cells as her new home and to disregard the outbursts of an envious policewoman.

Jeff is dismayed by the damaging disclosures flowing from Naomi and glances nervously at her. Maybe she is not the kind of catch he was expecting to net.

"What nature of business is Mr. Nyara and your O-T involved in?" Jeff asks Naomi suspiciously in a spiteful tone.

"Many!! Yesterday I overheard Adolf placing an order for water pumps. On-Top supplies merchandise for Nyara's hardware store. He is to deliver the pumps before tomorrow," Naomi speaks with naive pride of her brothers enterprising acumen and business contacts.

"Haa! Ha! Hoo! Ho! I see it all. You are a squadron of scavenging scoundrels, every one of you!" Jeff is up on his feet pointing accusing fingers at everybody in the cell and spitting coarse epithets to describe all occupants.

"*Sonko analeta rabsha, sumo! Budda anachokora mzinga wa nyuki?*" Gathimba is up, challenging Jeff for his verbal assault, terming it as poking his naked head in a bee hive. In the process, he sighs and exhales heavily close to Jeff's face. Jeff immediately, and with brutal force, pushes him away in disgust. Gathimba staggers left, right, but regains his balance and rambles around screaming.

"*Asali! Asali! Utalamba asali leo!*" he then whizzes out to fetch 'honey' for Jeff to sample, so he shouts.

"*Unaona sasa! Cheki muhadhara, nani atatuliza* Gathimba, *wewe* Manager *fala sana!*" Sumo ridicules Jeff for arousing Gathimba's filthy fury, and wondering who is going to contain him.

"Basoli *enda umsikize. Shika ndom umuchome atulie!*" Sumo acts cunningly, handing over a roll of bang to Basoli, who follows Gathimba to the toilets, aware dope will cool his nerves.

"*Poleni sana, sii hivo wazee! Nimemsukuma juu ya kunuka mdomo,*" Jeff is apologizing for violently shoving Gathimba and igniting his wrath. He pleads: the stench of Gathimba's breath was too revolting to withstand. Naomi walks back to her cell in a contemptuous cat walk swagger, an obvious snub to Jeff's advances.

Doors open!

"Supper! *Msosi! Sembe!*" Sumo reminds us it is evening meal. He walks out to receive Man Kariz our caterer.

Basoli and Gathimba are back in the cell before the steel doors open.

"*Wewe* Manager *wacha kasheshe na mezesha. Hapa ni jela, na sisi wote ni wapangaji wa Gava!*" Gathimba warns Jeff to ease on his sneering attitude towards others, because in jail, we are all, tenants of the state.

The evening diet is similar in colour, layout and aroma as lunch. Sumo is up to his task and embarks in serving the food.

Man Kariz summons Naomi to join the feast. This will be an opportune moment for me to talk to Naomi and get a message across to O-T, informing him of our tragedy. I need to alert him we cannot deliver the water pumps.

"Man Kariz! *Unamezea huyo manzi ni tasis wa On-Top, ule waa* Key-base Harlem?" Sumo updates the caterer on the unfolding news. The Beauty is sister to O-T.

"*Wacheni vako! Tasis wa O-T, naa inaweza kuwa kweli. On-Top nimemcheki ametuliza hapo nje!*" astonished by the sensational gossip, Man Kariz, apparently does not doubt Sumo's words, he has seen O-T hovering in the precincts of the police station.

"On-Top *yuko hapo nje!*" I exclaim in a wild optimistic gusto, praying O-T' will be the light leading out of this dark tunnel. Man Kariz is infuriated by my rowdy gimmicks and looks vexed.

Sumo apportions the food in seven bowls favouring two with a top layer of cabbage stew and choice chunks of the vegetable. Naomi enters the cell, settling between me and Jeff.

"*Gota sister! Gota! O-T yuko yadi! Anakushugulikia,*" Man Kariz greets Naomi with lustful eyes, extending his clenched fist and consoling her, saying On-Top is frantically seeking her release. Naomi almost hugs the caterer, motivated by his soothing sentiments. She clings to his hand mumbling messages meant for Simon Mwamba.

"Naomi! please, *tumana kwa O-T aambiwe maboys wake Pato na Marto tuko ndani,*" I attempt to pull Naomi aside and, speaking in a low tone, I beg her to pass a message to On-Top. I was to supply him with water pumps, but now we are behind bars, we need his help!

Woe unto us! Naomi treats me like the plague, cringing away fearfully and sporting a harassed expression on her face. She turns to Man Kariz to protect her from my presumed stalking. Man Kariz hits to impress, unleashing a vicious smack across my sore face. It sends me sprawling on the concrete surface.

"*Wewe chokora! Heshimu wakubwa wako! Na kaa kando. Unamshika shika nini!*" Man Kariz thinks I am an insult to my elders and sternly orders me to lay my hands off the Beauty. The slap painfully dims my hopes of soliciting On-Top's astute conspiracy antics to pull us out of these tribulations.

CHAPTER SEVEN

Sumo and Man Kariz depart for their covert transactions in the stinking washrooms. Jeff and Naomi are still on a food boycott, enabling Basoli and Gathimba to still parade bowlfuls of cabbages and stiff porridge.

"*Wewe chokora! Wacha mezesha!*" Naomi rebukes me for my expose on her brother. "*Usijaribu kutaja simo tena, ati unasema* water pumps. *Ushaiona* water pump *wewe*? *Perepepe mingi sare!*" She bars me in an intimidating tone not to mention O-T's name whilst insinuating that I have never seen a water pump.

Naomi has undergone a strange character and countenance metamorphosis, her true crafty characteristics well complementing the lifestyle here. She majestically strides out of the cell.

"Ummh! sliding off, like a sleazy imp!" Jeff says with a screwed up expression on his face, aggrieved by Naomi's snobbery and invigorated self-worth. "Compared to our Constable Wakesho, she is a frog," Jeff whispers and laughs sarcastically.

Overwhelmed with despair, I lose my appetite for the food. Martin seems oblivious of the worsening scenario and is busy savouring his bowlful of starch and greens.

"Son! Which school do you attend?" Jeff inquires in a fatherly tone. He presents me with another opportunity to interrogate him.

"After Tana Primary School, I did not join high school because of lack of money, but I still live in Huruma. Which particular place in Huruma did you most frequent, in your heydays?" I am desperate for his answers and my inquisitive probing urgency makes him withdraw in suspicion.

"Five thirty, and am still here! These people must be wishing for my death?" Jeff's cries for freedom and with nerves jerked by my prodding questions, he cannot bear being caged any more. Jeff rises up, scans his surroundings scornfully, shakes his head and walks out.

The sharp sound of knuckles knocking on the steel doors reverberates alarmingly in the stuffy cells.

"*Afande! Afande! Afande!*" Jeff is shouting while rapping on the door and attempting to capture the attention of the duty officer. His noisy action sends Sumo and Man Kariz scampering back into the cell.

Gathimba and Basoli are also jolted by the sharp knock on the metal doors as they gobble their food with apparent greed. Basoli almost throws up, shocked at Jeff's audacity to summon the cops.

Naomi walks in, her interest still on Man Kariz, "Please! Man Kariz *kumbuka maji; hapa sina haraka! Nitatoboa. Mimi nimezaliwa ghetto,*" Naomi reminds the caterer to smuggle in bottled water. She speaks with a courageous attitude of girl bred in the ghetto, she so reckons.

"*Huyu Sonko ana muhadhara mbaya mbovu!*" Man Kariz is flabbergasted by Jeff's audacious (or more aptly) publicity stunt and hurriedly starts gathering his crockery.

"*Haka kabuda hakana bahati OCS ashakitowa, hawezi toka leo ata akipiga nduru.*" The caterer discloses that the only officer authorised to release inmates – the Officer Commanding the Station (OCS) - has signed off from duty. Therefore Jeff's gimmicks will end up as noisy theatrics. He cannot be set free today.

The news will be devastating to Jeff who is positively adamant he will sleep in his warm bed tonight. The unlocking sound of the steel doors now resonates musically within the cells.

"*Unataka nini wewe! Usigonge huu mlango tena! Mjinga wewe!*" Wakesho's voice, harsh as it is, is a welcome relief from the present monotony. She reprimands Jeff for his foolish behaviour and warns him to stay away from the door.

"My Lawyer was here today. He promised me I will be released before the end of the day. It is nearly sundown. Can I please talk to the OCS, please Madam. My name is Jeff Riga," he pleads his case.

"Shame on you! You molest women coworkers during the day and expect to spend nights in the cosy arms of your wife. Sorry! Monday, is your day in court!" Wakesho retorts back at Jeff.

"*Alaa! Una saa na viatu! Tooaa! Tooaa! Na mshipi pia! Toa zote!*" Constable Wakesho has noticed Jeff has shoes on and still spots a watch on his wrist. She orders him to remove all the restricted wear.

We all scramble to the cell door, eager to witness the unfolding spectacle. In spite of Jeff begging on his knees, Wakesho remains obstinate, directing him to remove all the gear as per the cell rules. He strips the belt, shoe and watch reluctantly, as peeping faces giggle maliciously from the cell door.

Man Kariz has collected all the used bowls and excuses himself, "*Waathii! Tuonane kesho ngware!*" saying he will be back at dawn.

Constable Wakesho, after confiscating the items from Jeff shoves Naomi back into her lone cell and locks it. Thereafter, the main cell doors are loudly shut, sealing our fate for the day to enjoy the 'comfort' of the cold cell floor overnight. Jeff has been humbled by Wakesho and sits dejected, looking vulnerable in his corner.

"Rape *ni kisanga nooma, unafinywa uzazi! Ndiyo usiweze hiyo kazi tena,*" Gathimba has no consoling words for Jeff. He reckons a new law states rapists will henceforth be castrated.

"*Wapii! Unafungwa maisha!*" Basoli objects to Gathimba's assertions. He swears the change in law states that rapists are to be jailed for life.

"*Mafala nyinyi wotee, mimi namezea sheria!* Rape *siku hizi wanakufinya uzazi halafu wanakunyonga!*" Sumo is shocked at their ignorance of legal issues. He is well informed on judicial matters and submits: a convicted rapist is castrated and then hanged.

The trio hold back no qualms, as they paint a gloomy future for our Manager. I sincerely empathize with this gentleman, who I suspect is my father.

"*Na sisi je?*" Martin asks what portends for our offence.

"*Kisanga chenu ni toy! Mkisomewa mashtaka endeni kama mmekubali. Miaka yenu itabidi mpelekwe wamumu!*" Sumo advises us to plead guilty if taken to court. As minors, the magistrate will have no option but to send us to a reform school.

"*Lakini! Rondema lazima mfike,*" Basoli delivers a debilitating blow to our enthusiasm; we will not escape the dreaded Kamiti remand prison.

"*Mkubali kesi au mkatae. Kamiti! Rondema! lazima kabla mpelekwe wamumu, na huko sasa ndiyo kifo!*" Basoli persists in envisaging grim time ahead for Martin and me. A brief stint in the notorious remand prison of Kamiti, before we are placed in a reformatory school. The former, he says, will definitely 'kill' us.

Their revelations are shattering to both of us. The evening temperatures drop rapidly, cooling further the already cold cell as swarms of mosquitoes buzz overhead; an orchestra of what lies ahead of us.

CHAPTER EIGHT

"John Patrick Njeri! John Patrick Njeri!" Rotich's voice rings out, steering me out from a drowsy reverie.

"Yes Sir! Yes Sir!" I quickly gather my thoughts and rush out anticipating freedom. A bright light from the reception area blinds my approach along the dingy corridor.

Constable Rotich is at the front desk, while a tall, well-groomed man whose countenance can aptly be classified as grandfatherly, stands behind the counter. To my bewildering shock, standing besides him, is my mother.

"Mr. Nyara, *ile chokora anayeiba kwako ndiyo hii. Kaa chini chokora! Tabia na harufu kama ya fisi!*" Rotich introduces me to Mr. Nyara, as the scavenger stealing from his property, comparing me to a hyena, in both smell and behaviour. Then he orders me to sit on the floor.

"I know the boys' mother; Njeri, from way back when I used to reside in Huruma. Everybody knows I own property there!" Mr. Adolf Nyara speaks, his tone a rich baritone, an exuberance of his wealth. "Njeri *sikujua una kijana mkubwa hivi, na baba yuko wapi?*" Mr. Nyara seemingly well-acquainted with my mother, looking perplexed, and wondering where my father is.

"*Sijui kwa hakika, lakini! Ni wewe au Jeff rafiki yako. Mmoja wenu ndiye baba ya huyu chokora!*" my mother stuns the small assembly. Her candid confession on the possible identity of my father has me thunderstruck! One of them, Old Adolf here or flamboyant Jeff, is my probable father! Though mother is not certain who between the two is the real biological father, casting serious doubts on her morality before my birth.

"This hogwash rogue cannot be my son woman!" Nyara screams with a thunderous voice, which sends everybody cowering.

A strong whirlwind engulfs the reception area scattering all the paper on the desk. Rotich scrambles to restore order.

"*Rudisha yeye ndani, lazima DNA test ifanywe! Arudi ndani!*" Nyara roars that I should immediately be put back into the cells to await a DNA paternity test.

"*Sawa! Ni sawa! Chokora si shida yangu pekee, arudi ndani!*" my mother concurs with Mr. Nyara that I should be returned to the cells. She reckons this *chokora* scourge is not her creation alone and both walk away!

"*Amka! Amka, rudi ndani!*" Rotich jostles me to return to the holding cell, kicking me hard in my bruised ribs.

*****

"*Amka! Pato! Amka! Pato!*" It is Martin's voice at this instant. He is nudging me to wake up.

"*Hesabu! Pato kumekucha amka!*" Martin shakes me awake. It is roll call hour. It dawns on me, I was in a nightmare. It is Sunday morning and I am cuddled on the cold concrete surface of Jogoo Road Police Station.

Though warmly dressed in an oversized dirty hooded sweater, my body is stiff cold as I lazily orientate myself. The atmosphere is sombre with everyone crawling out of sleep like zombies in a human zoo.

"Out! *Kila mutu nje!*" it is the soothing soprano sound of Wakesho's voice commanding us to assemble for roll call. My face is painfully dotted with mosquito bites, with a vast number of the stinging insects flying into my mouth whenever I yawn. The early morning chilly breeze blowing from without eases the agony of the stink from within the cells.

Naomi stands outside her cell, a pale shadow of the elegant lady of the previous day. A night in a police cell has had a revolutionary overhaul of her beauty. Wearing no make up, with clothes and face wrinkled, she passes for a witch.

Wakesho is brief with the counting exercise. The clock at the reception area reads 05:30 hours, as she walks out.

"*Wazee* breakfast *ni saa ngapi?*" Jeff howls in hunger. He yearns for something to break his fast from the repugnant food which he shunned the previous day.

"*Sonko! Gota! Gota! Sonko! Maubao zimekubamba!*" Sumo salutes Jeff with his clenched fist. Excited, the manager is slowly adjusting to the deplorable environment, its inhabitants and now, the food. Jeff joyfully anticipates breakfast in a jail cell. Basoli and Gathimba follow suit, applauding Jeff for his gesture of solidarity.

"*Hata mimi chai nitakunywa,*" Naomi echoes similar sentiments. She is also starving. We all gather in our cell like a big happy family.

"Clink! Clank! Bang!" It is the opening doors. "*Chai wazee!* Man Kariz *amewasili,*" Sumo the pioneer prisoner announces the arrival of morning tea.

The plastic mugs for the dawn beverage are in no better shape or colour compared to the bowls used for the earlier meals. Man Kariz holds a polythene bag bulging with loaves of bread

Sumo, fast as ever, is on hand to serve the tea contained in a plastic bucket as Man Kariz clings to the bread, awaiting all to be served with the tea. Jeff and Naomi hastily grab the first plastic mugs and swiftly sip the hot liquid. The taste or the temperature of the tea seems to twist and curl their face masks but that does not deter them from sipping on.

Man Kariz shares the loaves discriminatingly, giving Sumo and his henchmen double portions.

"*Maji vipi Kariz, naa O-T mlibonga?*" Naomi inquires if the caterer has sneaked in bottled water; she also needs a feedback from On-Top.

"*Ni Noma! Mambo ni mbaya! Naomi, umeandikiwa* robbery with violence!" Man Kariz moans for Naomi. Her prospects appear bleak. To put it simply, she is in a sticky situation. Her offence: Robbery with Violence.

"*Wakesho alileta mezesha deadly! Alifukuza O-T, akasema haukubaliwi kuonwa na mtu, kesi yako ni ya mavedi,*" Man Kariz reveals Wakesho hounded On-Top out from the station precincts claiming visitors are barred from seeing Naomi. Her offence is being investigated by the incorruptible arm of police detectives. The news is distressing to Naomi who immediately loses her zest for the unpleasant bland brew served as tea.

"*Nipee namba ya O-T. Mimi najulikana sana, hata OCS mimi naweza mwingiza box! Ngoja utaona!*" Man Kariz speaks well. All he requires is On-Top's phone number, as customary with the minions in our society. Man Kariz brags of his importance and abilities, suggesting he can place the Officer in charge of the police station under his spell, thus assuring Naomi to entrust her fate upon him.

"*Chukua number ya mzee wangu, Adolf, anamezea mavedi wote, na umshow ulcers zinaniumiza, atumane dawa,*" Naomi opts to provide Mr. Nyara's contacts, for he is well-acquainted with all arms of the police force or so she claims. Hands on her tummy, she is wincing in pain. Her act of agony and desperation is 'award winning'. We all empathise with her hurting stomach ulcers. The whole cell is mumbling curses aimed at Naomi's adversaries, and from the glare of all our faces, all desire to provide her with a shoulder to cry on.

Her mention of Mr. Nyara reminds me of the disturbing dream earlier and our brief encounter, meanwhile I routinely scrutinize Jeff from his forehead to his big toe, hoping he fits into my perceived portrait of my father. As for Nyara's demand for a paternity test he ought to be analyzed with Sumo.

Man Kariz packs his wares ready to depart.

"Pastor Moses Ajabu *atakuja kuhubiri leo, hakikisha amekuwekelea mikono ili utoe nooks, Naomi! Sawa!*" Man Kariz alerts us, a certain Pastor Ajabu will be conducting a cell service today. He advises Naomi to seek the clerics divine intervention, lay his holy hands on Naomi, to keep off any taboos.

"*Sawa Kariz, na wewe please! Jaribu kuongea na Adolf, nisikufie huku ndani,*" Naomi agrees with Man Kariz, but urges him to plead her case before Mr. Nyara, fearing the deplorable conditions in jail will surely kill her.

"*Ati* Pastor Ajabu *atakuja hapa leo?*" Jeff is terrified a Pastor will be evangelizing here today. "Pastor Moses Ajabu of Mighty Miracles will be ministering here today! He cannot find me here!" Jeff is in panic, his stomach rumbles loudly while letting out foul air from his rear. It all sounds like a stalled tractor.

Jeff, with one hand on the stomach and the other on his behind, dashes out to the toilets, leaving us overwhelmed with laughter. The practice here, before visiting the toilets, is to borrow the second footwear from cell mates, as all spot one shoe on their feet. Jeff has ignored the rule. The flooded toilets will definitely water down his miseries.

Soon after the caterer is ushered out, the steel doors open again. It must be Pastor Moses Ajabu, wearing a black suit and carrying a briefcase. He is escorted into our cell by Constable Rotich, who I presume is here to declare his presence as the duty officer and physically ascertain all prisoners are secured.

"*Mnajisi yuko wapi?*" Rotich asks sarcastically the whereabouts of the 'rapist', referring to Jeff.

"*Choo! Amekimbia kwa choo,*" Gathimba answers that Jeff is holed up in the toilets.

"*Nikiwa kati ya kondoo wangu niko nyumbani. Unaweza tuwacha sasa!*" Pastor Ajabu speaks graciously. He now feels at home and is geared to shepherd his flock, dismissing Rotich.

I have failed to mention Pastor Ajabu is accompanied by a beautiful young lady, dressed in a flowing colourful African *kitenge* dress, and clutching onto a Bible. Jeff returns, and stands still at the cell entrance, as his eyes lock onto Pastor Moses Ajabu, who also turns to meet his gaze.

CHAPTER NINE

"Baba Tania! What are you doing here?" Pastor Ajabu is shocked to see Jeff. "Your phone is off, I called your wife and she told me you are out of town. What is happening?" The perplexed Pastor asks Jeff, formally referring to him as Tania's father.

"Yes! I told your sister, I am in Mombasa. You know women! They are always nagging and snooping around for any slip ups. I had to escape with this lie after a cock up at the supermarket," Jeff defends his presence in the cells, with a shy and embarrassed demeanour as he enters the cell and takes his position.

"Let us forgive so as we can be forgiven, brothers and sisters!" the Preacher begins his sermon, introducing his female companion as Sister Lucy of Mighty Miracles Prison Outreach Programme.

"Our Mission is to rescue souls from the shackles of sin," says the captivating cleric, fishing out a black bible from his briefcase.

"Your fathers and mothers have failed you!" he continues, directly addressing Martin and I.

"The young have lost hope and shun spirituality," his eyes on Sumo and compatriots.

"Immorality is fashionable and a vocation to many!" a barb aimed at Naomi.

"Fathers cannot be trusted or adored as role models," Ajabu preaches on, an obvious reference to Jeff and the entire congregation. Sister Lucy claps on her bible excitedly, shouting favourable praise words over the admonitions directed at the cell occupants.

"*Wacheeni perepepe mingi, Mungu wangu yuko huko milimani! Wacheni kutu-enjoy mimi sii faala! mambo ya dini namezea!*" Gathimba interrupts the sermon, castigating the Pastor for trumpeting his message! Declaring his God resides in the mountains and tells the duet to stop taking us for a ride, while swearing he is not stupid in spiritual matters.

"*Tukitoe! Tukavute* herb, *hawa ni wakereketo waa kanisa za jaro!*" Sumo prefers to get stoned and signals his two accomplices to join him in the toilets, terming the pious pair as dubious religious campaigners.

Pastor Ajabu is not deterred by these 'satanic' sideshows and strongly surges ahead with his sermon.

"Time is now! Here today, accept change and get saved," the persuasive pastor persists, to an all attentive flock after the departure of the 'treacherous trio'. Moses Ajabu is your typical new age pastor still in his youth. His testimony sheds light to a troubled past of drunkenness and debauchery. Now reformed, he is a crusader for the ideal citizen and the good in society.

"To crown this service, all who are willing to take the leap of salvation, please stand up so I can lay my hands on you," he advocates for a concluding act of conversion. Naomi, Jeff and I are touched by his moving discourse and take our spots faithfully. I pray to be set free from the burdens of my trespasses.

Martin is seated and skeptical of my new venture. He opts to skip the ritual. Sister Lucy closes the session with a tearful emotional homily, welcoming us to their family. Thereafter, Pastor Ajabu rummages through his brief case and fetches out three blue pocket bibles, handing one to each of us.

"May this be your road map to a new life as you walk in the light of the words herein," the preacher speaks as he presents the Bibles. The brand new holy book emits a delicious fresh smell, which refreshes my battered taste buds.

Martin looks tempted to extend his hand for the free bibles but is embarrassed. Pastor Ajabu notices his covetous yearnings and offers him a copy.

The three racketeers return and appear possessed as they stagger into the cell. They are sluggish in their movements. All three spot bloodshot eyes! They manage to collapse appropriately in their various positions.

Pastor Ajabu pulls Jeff aside and whispers a silent prayer before moving out. I presume it is in pursuit of other lost sheep trapped in similar dungeons.

"*Mmetubu dhambi zenu! Sasa nataka* cell *ing'are kama hiki kiatu changu!* OCS *anakuja* inspection, *mtu wa kuosha choo yuko karibu kufika!*" Rotich standing by the doorway appreciates we have repented our transgressions, orders us to clean up the cell and make it sparkle like his military boots. The Officer Commanding Station will be conducting an inspection shortly.

Luckily and hygienically for us, the cleaning of the toilets has been assigned to a hired hand from outside and not us in the cells.

Martin and I are nonetheless obliged to do the task of cleaning as all the others move into Naomi's cell. A broom, bucket full of water and a mucky rug are the tools available to shine the cells and corridor. We do this as Rotich paces back and forth between the reception area and the cells supervising the clean-up.

Out of the blue, the hired hand makes his grand entrance! He is fully equipped to clean the reeking toilets. He is also dressed for the occasion.

"*Papaa! Umeingia! Kazi ni kazi, mchagua jembe sio mkulima! Papaa wewe shikilia kazi!*" constable Rotich, aware of the revolting toils of the hired hand offers some consolation to the guy he calls Papaa. Rotich comforts him with a past popular proverb which loosely translates 'beggars are not choosers', and a job on hand is without doubt the right job as long as it pays a wage.

Papaa is in blue overalls and black gumboots carrying a toilet pump, a bucket filled with detergent and a big mop. He is a short, fat, balding, middle-aged man. He smiles broadly at Rotich's polite acclaim of his role in society, and enthusiastically walks on to perform his unpleasant chores.

After a repetitive procedure of moping and drying the depleted floors, Rotich frowns with contentment and declares the cell floors are finally glittering in uniformity with his police boots.

From the toilets, Papaa surely aims at perfection, for as he walks away, the pervasive stench is gone. There is a sombre mood along the cold corridor as we all take a well-deserved breather. Sumo, Basoli and Gathimba, wallowing in a miasma of drugged motions also stretch out their limbs in delight at the invigorated ambience.

The steel door which is slightly shut now opens wide. An imposing gentleman, wearing a well-pressed police uniform, looms large. He displays an authoritative disposition and holds a wooden cane in his left palm. Constable Rotich appears and stands still next to him, while holding onto the Occurrence Book.

"*Kaba! Kila mtu kaba mstari mmoja!*" Rotich shouts out, a dreaded directive asking that all to squat in a single file. The distinguished officer must be the much hyped OCS. He strides forward. His name tag reads Chief Inspector Abdi, his rank confirmed by the six stars gracing his shoulder lapels.

An extended gesture of his arm and Rotich passes him the Occurrence Book, which also acts as the cell register.

"Walter Thomas Aduda, alias, Sumo!" Inspector Abdi calls out the name after perusing through the big book.

"Yes Sir!" Sumo answers, standing up.

"Paul Stanely Midau, also known as, Basoli!" Officer Abdi also summons Sumo's co-accused.

"*Niko Afande!*" Basoli responds, jumping onto his feet.

"You two have turned my surrounding neighbourhoods into your mugging fields. Tomorrow you will be charged in court for robbing a blind woman of her expensive mobile phone. I am positive she identified you through your nauseating scent!" Chief Inspector Abdi speaks with a tone of disdain, appalled by the goons' crime.

"Gathimba wa Kamau! You are a local terrorist and touting for passengers at the bus park is a mere masquerade gimmick. You will also be in court tomorrow, charged with belonging to an outlawed sect".

All three meekly seem to accept their fate as the senior officer orders them to continue squatting.

"John Patrick and Martin Joseph, *Simama juu!*" the senior officer loudly commands us to stand up. "I am tempted to whack your backsides, but this cane is too precious and expensive to be soiled," Inspector Abdi speaks with compassion while firmly slapping the cane on his right leg viciously.

I am also told you both are fatherless. Nonetheless, I expect your mothers to be here today, otherwise you will both face a magistrate tomorrow morning," he dismisses us with a contemptuous gesticulation of his polished cane.

"Naomi Njoki! For choosing cannibalism to settle scores, your offence is still under investigation with our top detectives. So stay put for interrogation tomorrow!" he further drowns Naomi's quest for freedom.

"Jeff Riga! Your lawyer posted bail yesterday, you will be released immediately I sign the necessary paperwork," Chief Inspector Abdi concludes his inspection tour. Thereafter, he hands back the book to Rotich and walks away while reciprocating the junior officer's salute gesture.

CHAPTER TEN

He is without doubt the man of the moment. Jeff is basking in the glory of his pending release from this confinement as we assemble in our cell. Naomi is beaming with vitality as she tags besides him. We are all seeking his attention.

"*Tulieni! Tulieni! Nitasikiza kila mtu! Tulieni!*" Jeff with the tact of a politician controls the small crowd craving for his attention, promising to gratify all our wishes.

Jeff is ecstatic at the unfolding scenario and embraces Naomi's overtures with open arms, pulling her to his corner. His 'scavenger' instincts appear to be having the better of him. All need his favour to communicate with the outside world. Naomi side-steps us all, and is the first to submit her supplications.

"Oooh! Jeff! Please! Talk to Nyara. You told me, he is like a brother to you. I promise to compensate you for your efforts. I have some money stashed somewhere!" Naomi cajoles him, with a weird wink.

"The moment I step out of this quagmire, I will call Mr. Nyara and you will be out of here pronto! Cast your burdens unto me!" Jeff brags, as he consoles her.

"*Ma-boys wangu! Home ni wapi? Huruma naijua yote!*" Jeff is still sympathetic of our dilemma and is willing to go the extra mile to trace our homes in Huruma. My grandmother had been a major supplier of a popular illicit brew in the early days. People still refer to our residence as *Depoti* a corruption of 'The Depot'. She has since quit the trade.

"*Unajua Depoti, Huruma, katikati, hapo ndiyo home,*" I navigate him through Huruma in reference to 'The Depot'.

"*Depoti, aah! Kwa ule matha wa chang'aa, huyo matha ananijua mzuri sana!*" Jeff excitedly admits he is in familiar grounds; he has even met my grandmother. She brewed the cheap liquor popularly called *chang'aa* by locals. Her distilling skills were legendary in Huruma, so am told. Jeff, acknowledging he is conversant with my neighbourhood, strengthens my intuition that he is my biological father.

Martin's home is only a short distance from my house and Jeff assures us he will do everything possible to reach our guardians before today's deadline.

"Your mothers must be here today!" the booming and commanding voice of Chief Inspector Abdi resounds chillingly in my head! I silently pray my mother shocks Jeff with the ultimate revelation that I am his son.

Gathimba has also been humbled by the OCS' assertions. He will be in court tomorrow. "*Buda! Nataka upigie machali wa Kamjesh simu, uwashow niko huku!*" Gathimba wishes to provide Jeff with the telephone contacts of his touting cartel buddies, soliciting for their help. He migrated to the city recently and has no close relatives to bail him out.

Sumo is amused by our efforts to petition Jeff and disrupts Gathimba's talk.

"*Mafala nyinyi wote! Sonko anawatoshanisha. Akitoka hapa hamtamskia tena. Mimi buda niwachie ile unaniwachia!*" Sumo posits that Jeff's act of compassion is only a circus to hoodwink us. Sumo reckons the guy will disappear the moment he steps out of the cell. However, even so, Sumo demands an exit fee from him. Jeff, caressing his small bible between his hands, ignores Sumo's negative jibes.

"*Achote! Sonko achote kabla atoke. Anafikiria tutakula nini rondema,*" Basoli concurs with Sumo, insisting the 'exit levy' is a bonus for their upkeep at the dreaded Kamiti remand prison.

The opening doors provide Jeff with an opportune moment to recollect his thoughts from the duos' extortion bombardments. He hastens to the door, hoping this is his moment of liberation.

"*Yaaakk! Ni Man Kariz na mitungi za msosi!*" Jeff turns back in disgust. It is the caterer carrying his food containers.

"Manager *wa manyeege! Nasikia unatoka. Lakini msosi lazima ukule. Ulikuwa ushahesabiwa!*" Man Kariz follows Jeff's withdrawal into the cells with spiteful words, labelling him a sex pest. Though he is set to be released, rules stipulate he has to eat the lunch for his portion was included, so asserts the caterer.

Sumo is still obsessed with serving meals and immediately relieves Man Kariz of his catering tools. He embarks on the task with zest.

"*Naomi! Huyu sonko wako hapatikani! Simu yake nii mteja!*" Man Kariz's courier assignment for Naomi has yielded nought. He cannot find Mr. Nyara.

Naomi cannot stomach Man Kariz's failure and prefers to give him the cold shoulder. Having found another listening ear, she is now fixated on Jeff.

"*Buda! Achote! Sumo! Buda achote!*" Basoli is not yet through with Jeff, reminding Sumo of their extortion exercise. Sumo is absorbed with his undertaking. He is jolted by the evocation of a monetary shakedown on Jeff. He holds high, a big serving spoon, and glares at him.

"*Wewee buda tuwachie kitu!*" Sumo yells menacingly at Jeff for a kickback.

"Chapaa nimeandikisha kwa kitabu. Nikitoka nitawachia Man Kariz" Jeff, sensing brewing animosity, quickly assures them. Their bribe is forthcoming, he says He has deposited money at the station's front desk. Man Kariz will act as the conduit to channel their reward soon after his release.

"Man Kariz *unasikia, usimwache! Lazima achote!"* Sumo urges the *Caterer* to keep close tabs on Jeff after his release, to obtain the inducement.

As soon as Basoli and Gathimba settle to devour their bowlfuls of cabbage broth and *ugali*, Jeff and Naomi stage a walk out. They leave behind their apportioned bowls of food. As usual, the scorn is a delight to the two gluttons who transfer the spurned meals into their own bowls. Sumo has sufficiently stuffed his bowl with extra helpings and smiles as he finds the appropriate posture to enjoy his heap.

Martin seems withdrawn as he eats. Our incarceration has severely diminished his self-esteem, aware I can no longer provide a solution to the current crisis. I am also overwhelmed by these wretched surroundings and the gloomy prospects facing us. I look at Martin and my mind goes back to the morning of our partnering.

******

Within Huruma you will find Nairobi's largest goat market. It is a cluster of slaughter houses famously known as *Kia-Maiko*. In a wanton search for cheap labour, unscrupulous goat traders employ young children from our neighbourhood to clean animal waste. Hunger, due to the poverty at home, led Martin to the unpalatable job of sweeping goat droppings from the transport trucks. He lives with his single mother and two elder siblings in a much smaller room compared to this cell. I was a fully-fledged scavenger when I met Martin six years ago.

I remember the morning was, as usual, shivering cold as I made my way through the rough paths leading out of Huruma. He was the shortest in a pack of boys jostling for a cleaning job from a pot-bellied, stout fellow busy chewing the intoxicating popular twig called *mogoka*. I felt pity for the hustling boys, knowing they earned a pittance for the filthy job. The trader pulled aside three of the tallest and strongest from the group and dismissed the rest.

On-Top, my scavenging partner and mentor, had recently moved out of Huruma. I have been operating solo recently and the rejected lads present me with an opportunity to recruit another partner. During my first outing with Martin, loitering in the Eastlands suburbs and collecting trashed items which we sold to a scrap metal dealer, we managed to make five hundred shillings. Martin had never seen so much money in his life. From that day on, he became my disciple.

Our escapades are a secret from family and neighbours, especially the girls. After a busy day of scavenging, we visit the public showers at the Huruma field grounds before going home neatly clean. Our mothers appreciate our efforts to make an extra buck and never question the source of our money.

*****

The now familiar sound of unlocking metal doors cuts short my calm as Man Kariz hurriedly gathers his utensils ready to depart.

"*Jeff Riga! Jeff Riga, kuja na kila kitu chako!*" Rotich's voice speaks freedom for Jeff, reminding him not to leave anything behind. Jeff Riga is as slippery as an eel. He is out of Naomi's cell before we can recollect our thoughts, disrupted by the opening doors. I was hoping to further plead for his help, but peeping through the corridor, I only catch a glimpse of Man Kariz disappearing out.

63

I return to my position with a feeling of despair and notice the blue pocket bible presented to Jeff, lying close by. In a desperate dash to freedom he has abandoned his road map to a new life.

As the steel doors slam and shut, it is yet another painful sound, spelling my doom.

Translation of Kiswahili/Sheng Words Used in the Book

CHAPTER ONE

Na Mukae gaangari	Stay Alert
Msiolewe	Do not get married
Huko Ndani	Inside there
Chokora	Scavenger
Amaka	Arise
Mmsare	Leave him/her
Mwaache	Leave him/her
Hawa	These
Wanakujua	Do they Know
Nani	Who
Mafalaa	Idiots
Mtaa	Neighbourhood
Sonko	Wealthy Person/Boss
Kitu Kidogo	Something small
Soo Moja	One Hundred Kenya Shillings
Chotaa	Hand over
Kabuda	Old Man
Kanarudi	Coming back
Wazimu	Mad

CHAPTER TWO

Cucu	Grandmother
Twende	Let's Go
Tuka-chome	Get stoned/high
Bamba	Hold It
Mungiki	A dreaded outlawed sect in Kenya
Mavi	Faeces

Muhadhara	Exposure
Bestee	Friend
Tuliza	Take it easy
Uwanja Mdogo	Small field
Kiboko	Whip
Motoni	On Fire

CHAPTER THREE

Wacha Pupaa	Stop worrying
Sisi Wote	All of us
Wapangaji	Tenants
Eleza	Tell/Narrate
Kisanga	Crime/Ordeal
Yenu	Yours
Paraa	Camouflage
Jaroo	To fool
Vaako	Pretend
Tupu	Empty
Nimaa	They are
Shetani	Evil
Wacheni	Leave it
Wataangamia	They will perish
Maskan	Hideout
Kusanya	To steal/gather
Lazima	Must
Ukae	Live
Ngumu	Hard
Nooma	Trouble
Hiiyo	That
Msosi	Food

CHAPTER FOUR

Uniite	Call Me
Ukimaliza	Upon finishing

Kuja	Come
Tuonane	We meet
Huku Ndani	Inside here
Maliza	Finish
Mangale	Cigarettes
Maboza	Marijuana
Manzi	Girl
Msuupa	Gorgeous
Kitoa	Gone
Ashindwe	Defeated
Kumbuka	Remember
Jioni	Evening
Wathii	Guys/Travelers
Huyo	That one
Mbuss	Lady/Girl
Bambiwa	Arrested
Sema	Say
Panganga	Chatter
Hatuwezani	We are not able
Nyeta	Snobbish
Mlambishe	Let him/her lick it
Gani	Which one
Natamani	I yearn
Rondema	Remand Prison
Horse Kobole	Five Hundred Kenya Shillings
Kameivaa	It has paid off
Tukavute	To smoke
Waiivee	Get high/stoned

CHAPTER FIVE

Ya Ma-babi	For the rich
Massangu	My Mother
Budda	Father
Sisi	Us

Hatuna	We do not have
Burungo	Package/Goods
Alikwachu	He/she took
Haku-nimezea	Did not recognize me

CHAPTER SIX

Una-hanya-hanya	Being promiscuous
Rabsha	Melee
Anachokora	Prodding
Mzinga wa nyuki	Bee Hive
Asali	Honey
Leo	Today
Ndom	Marijuana
Sembe	Thick porridge
Mezesha	Sell out
Tasis	Sister to
Nimemcheki	I have seen him/her
Ametuliza	Settled
Anakushugulikia	He/she looking out for you

CHAPTER SEVEN

Perepere Mingi	Too much chatter
Afande	Sir
Mbaya Mbovu	Too bad
Ashakitowa	Already gone
Unafinywa uzazi	You were castrated
Wamumu	Reform school

CHAPTER EIGHT

Mavedi	Crime detectives
Muingiza box	Cast a spell
Utoe nooks	Remove a curse

CHAPTER NINE

Wacheni	Leave it
Mingi	Too much
Namezea	I know
Wakereketo	Lobbyist/activist
Za jaro	Not real
Kila Mtu	Everybody
Kaba	Squat

CHAPTER TEN

Tulieni	Calm down
Nitasikiza	I will listen
Machali	Boys/ friends
Kamjesh	Touts
Anawatoshanisha	Fooling you
Achote	Hand over money
Kabla akitoe	Before leaving
Manyeege	Sexual arousal
Chapaa	Money
Ugali	Thick porridge